CHAD AND
THE ELEPHANT ENGINE

Weekly Reader Books presents

Illustrated by Judith Gwyn Brown

THE ELEPHANT ENGINE

Marjorie Filley Stover

Atheneum   New York   1975

To John,

who likes circuses

and trains

Text copyright © 1975 by Marjorie Filley Stover
Illustrations copyright © 1975 by Judith Gwyn Brown
All rights reserved
Published simultaneously in Canada by
McClelland & Stewart, Ltd.
Manufactured in the United States of America

Library of Congress Cataloging in Publication Data

Stover, Marjorie Filley.
Chad and the elephant engine.
SUMMARY: A boy acrobat with the circus longs
to be an elephant boy.
[1. Circus stories] I. Brown, Judith Gwyn, illus.
II. Title. PZ7.S8889Ch [Fic] 74-19312
ISBN 0-689-30458-7

Contents

*This story is based
on one of the legends of
the Denver, South Park &
Pacific Railroad. Maybe
in 1887 or thereabouts.*

Acrobat Boy

CHAD SETTLED HIS FEET firmly on Poppa's broad shoulders. He looked up at the sheet of canvas above him. Then with a flick of his fingers, he sent the red ball up toward the top of the circus tent. The white ball followed and then the blue to the rhythm of the gay tune the band was playing.

Red, white, and blue, he kept them up and down in the air. Suddenly the loud trumpeting of an elephant sounded above the music. Wondering, Chad took his eyes off the balls. And in that half second he missed the red ball, and it came bouncing down on his father's head.

3

There was a bit of laughter from the crowd. He reached out in time to catch the white and blue balls, but a rosy flush spread over his face and neck. As he swung down, Poppa sputtered, "You going to be a clown maybe? Keep your eyes on the ball."

Chad's feet hit the sawdust, and he bounced back beside his father. As they took a quick bow, he tried to explain. "That elephant trumpet! Something's wrong!"

His father's words popped out angrily from under his walrus moustache. "Elephants, bah! You're an *acrobat* boy. Forget the elephants."

Chad blinked in surprise. Poppa sounded really upset. But there was no more time for talk. The band was swinging into the music for the next stunt.

Chad's mother and his two uncles, Carlos and Boots, leaped into the center of the ring. His uncles were not as big as Poppa, but they were as full of life as a pair of mountain lions, and as handsome.

Carlos winked an eye at Chad, and Boots drew the corners of his mouth down, to make

himself look sad. Mama, graceful in her pink tights, gave him a smile as she moved into her part. Chad felt better at once. He flipped into a backward handspring and finished the act with no more mistakes.

The acrobats bounded out on a wave of applause. Outside the tent Boots gave Chad's ear a friendly pull, and Carlos said, "Don't forget, I'll meet you right after the show." Off they hurried to change costumes.

Mama stopped only long enough for a feather-light kiss on Chad's cheek. "You were tops in the pyramid!" It was a little joke between them, and they both laughed. With a toss of her curly black hair, she hurried off. Mama had only a few minutes to tie a pink net ballet skirt over her tights and pick up her pink silk parasol for the slack-wire act.

Poppa should have hurried, too. Instead he stopped short, and his black eyes glared down at Chad. "An acrobat keeps his mind on his work. He isn't upset by an elephant trumpeting. When the show is over, you come back to the tent, practice your juggling—and your exercises."

Chad's heart dropped as fast as the ball he had missed. "Not right after the show! Carlos is going to town between shows. He promised I could go with him."

Poppa jabbed a finger at Chad. "Whether you like it or not, you're going to practice. There better not be any slipups in your part tonight—not if every animal in the circus is screaming." Poppa strode off, beating the ground with his feet.

Chad stood staring unhappily at the mountain peaks rising behind the circus tents, but he hardly saw them. Why had he missed that ball today of all days? The circus tents were only a few blocks from the town stores—close enough to walk. Circus lots were nearly always way out on the fringes of town. The circus moved so often from one place to the next that visits to the stores were a treat.

Usually Chad's only view of them was during the parade. From his perch high on the seat of a gaily painted wagon, he waved to the people who filled the streets. Behind the crowds were those exciting store windows. He could only get a quick look at the sturdy-handled picks and shovels, heavy ore buckets, rubber hip boots, miner's lamps, self-cocking revolvers, and tin pans for panning gold.

Chad had lived in the circus all of his life. However, until this summer he had never been in the mountains. The Colorado mining towns, resting in the valleys or hanging on the rocky slopes, were different from any towns he had ever known.

The discovery of silver and gold in the Rocky

Mountains had long ago brought a rush of fortune seekers. Now the towns were large and rich from the precious ore dug out of the hillsides. Unpainted board shacks, sturdy log cabins, and gingerbread-trimmed frame houses stood side by side along the winding dirt streets.

Now, all because he had missed a ball, Chad had to stay at the circus grounds and practice. He scowled at a long trail of smoke rising from the big building where the ore was treated to make it pure.

Practice, practice! That was all Poppa thought about. If only the ball hadn't hit Poppa's head and made people laugh. If only the elephant hadn't trumpeted just then.

Why was Poppa so down on the elephants?

Of all the animals, Queenie and Sheba were Chad's favorite. He was great friends, too, with Subhas, their trainer. Subhas could tell him story after story about India where he and the elephants had once lived.

The elephants were strong and clever. They helped set up the big circus tent and take it down. When a circus wagon became stuck in the mud, Queenie or Sheba would push it out. One of them alone could do what a team of eight horses pulling hard could not do.

When Chad was still quite small, Subhas had taught Queenie to curl her trunk so that Chad could sit in it. The elephant lifted him high in the air while he waved to the excited crowd.

Last spring Chad had been thrilled clear down to his toes when Subhas had asked him to help even more. *Dressing the act* was fun. He sat on Sheba's head, balanced on Queenie's back, or posed beside them as they did their tricks.

The more Chad did with the elephants, the more he wanted to do. Most of all he wished that *he* could be the one to give the commands. He knew all the Hindi words that Subhas used to make Queenie and Sheba do their tricks and help with the work. He liked the sound of the Hindi words. He liked the way they rolled off his tongue.

Chad kicked at a stone. The elephant had gotten him into trouble this time. No trip to town. He could hear the band playing "Oh! Susanna." No matter where he was, Chad could tell exactly what was happening inside the big tent by the music the band was playing. He better get into his costume for the elephant act.

He kicked another stone and headed for the pad room.

This was a long tent with the men's dressing space at one end, the women's at the other, and the horses in between. Chad's trunk was lined up with all the others around the room. It held his costumes, makeup box, and regular clothes.

Usually Chad felt happy and proud as he put on the blue satin suit. Not today. All the fun had gone out of the afternoon. Unhappily he wiggled into the baggy pants that tapered to a tight fit on his legs.

Poppa was cross as a bear these days. Other summers he had seemed glad enough to have Subhas tell stories to Chad. This summer the more time Chad spent with the elephants, the more upset Poppa became.

"You oughtta be using your free time to practice the juggling and acrobatic stunts," Poppa had shouted last time, his walrus moustache jabbing up and down with every word.

Mama's mouth had circled into a tiny pout. "Poppa! He's only a *little* boy."

Chad had squirmed. He didn't feel *that* little.

Poppa drew in a deep breath. His chest rose high and his eyes flashed with pride. "We're an *acrobat* family, Chad. One of the best in the business. Don't you forget it."

Chad had stared at Poppa. Of course, they were an acrobat family. How could he forget that? But he had only ducked his head and said, "Yes, Poppa." Then he had practiced a few cartwheels and backward somersaults; but soon he was back with the elephants.

Still unhappy, Chad buttoned on the blue satin coat with its high, round collar. He couldn't understand Poppa. All of the circus people did a number of different things. Poppa, Carlos, and Boots had a juggling act that kept the audience breathless. Poppa could keep six plates spinning and not break a single one.

Poppa was the star of a team of five leapers. They lined up and took turns running up a ramp, bouncing on a springboard, and flying through the air over an ever-growing number of horses. Each leaper landed on a mat, turned a somersault, and returned to the end of the line. One . . . two . . . three . . . four . . . five . . . six horses.

One by one the other leapers dropped out. Hank stopped at six. Boots stopped at seven. Pete and Carlos quit at eight. With a huge bounce on the springboard, Poppa leaped over *nine* horses.

Poppa rode in the Wild West Show. He was ground assistant to Mama in her slack-wire act.

Chad tied a sash around his waist and shoved his feet into red shoes that curled to a point over his toes. He stopped dressing and counted on his fingers. One way or another Poppa was in eight different acts.

Reaching into his trunk, Chad found his red satin turban and put it on his head. He hurried outside and saw Queenie and Sheba lumbering up to the entrance.

Subhas walked by Queenie's left front leg. Rufe, the new bull hand, walked by Sheba's left front leg. Chad looked enviously at Rufe. A bull hand got to stay with the elephants all of the time.

Chad Helps a Friend

THE AFTERNOON SHOW WAS over. Chad stood in the shadow of a tent, watching Carlos and Boots go across the field toward town. Half the circus people seemed to be headed for town. He saw Skeets and Rollo, the clowns, Dorinda and Don, the bareback riders, Carmen, Zorina, Doc, Rufe, Pete, Slim—even Mama and Poppa! It just wasn't fair.

They trailed in little groups across the field and along the railroad siding where the long string of yellow circus cars stood. The name, JINGLEHOFFER CIRCUS, was painted in big, red letters on each car.

16

The Jinglehoffer Circus might not be one of the biggest, but in a one-ring circus you were always the star when your act was on. Besides, Jinglehoffer's was one of the best. Everyone knew that a circus that traveled by railroad was much better than one that went in horse-drawn wagons.

Of course, the Denver, South Park & Pacific was a narrow-gauge railroad. The distance between the tracks was only three feet. That was to be expected in the mountains.

However, this afternoon not even the sight of the circus railroad cars could comfort Chad. He turned away. Eyes on the ground, he scuffed at the dirt, as he walked back to the show tent and into the ring.

Usually there were other circus people practicing. Not today. Rows of empty seats stretched around him. He slumped down on a front-row seat. He didn't *feel* like practicing, not when everyone else had gone to town.

Unhappily, Chad pounded a hand on the seat next to him. He reached out a foot and began scraping up a little pile of sawdust. Why shouldn't he work more and more with the elephants? he asked himself again.

Last week he was sure his chance had come. Subhas's helper had quit Saturday night as soon as the show was over. He had drawn his wages from Mr. Jinglehoffer and packed his duffel bag. There was a gleam in his eye. "I'm gonna quit this ragbag for good! Gonna find me a gold mine!" he had said, and tramped off with a gray-bearded prospector and his burro.

Chad had hoped he could be the one to help Subhas now. "I already know how," he had offered. "I know all the commands."

From under his brown turban Subhas had smiled gently and shaken his head. "Little Sahib belongs to acrobat family. A bull hand must stay with the elephants."

Subhas had chosen Rufe from among the roustabouts, the circus men who did the heavy work. Rufe was big and clumsy, but he liked the elephants.

Chad watched Subhas show Rufe how to strap on the elephant's work harness and how to fasten the velvet blankets for the parade. He watched while Subhas showed Rufe how to prod Sheba with the bull hook, a wooden stick with a metal hook in one end.

"Queenie and Sheba good elephants. No need to push hard enough to hurt much. Just hard enough they know you mean business," explained Subhas.

Rufe soon learned to do these things. However, he shook his head over the strange Hindi words Subhas used to command. "Way I figure it, the *elephants* ought to learn *English*," he said. "Why should I have to learn Hindi?"

Subhas's dark eyes had shone beneath his turban. "Hindi words not strange to Queenie and Sheba. You listen. Soon will not be strange to you."

"I'll help you, Rufe," Chad had offered. "*Utthao*. That means 'move ahead.' Now you try it. *Utthao*."

Rufe opened his mouth. "*U-u-u—*. My tongue won't talk like that," he had said shaking his head.

Chad stared down at the little mountain of sawdust piled up at his feet. Once more he wished that Subhas would give *him* a chance to order the elephants. With one swipe of his foot the sawdust mountain disappeared.

The wailing trumpet of an elephant tore the air again. What was the matter with those elephants? They had done their afternoon tricks well enough, but they had seemed upset. Subhas, too, had acted uneasy. He had been unusually quiet and had given only the necessary commands.

As a second trumpet followed the first, Chad leaped to his feet and raced outside. In spite of the sunshine, there was a cool breeze sweeping off the mountainside. Chad buttoned his sweater as he hurried past the red wagon that was Mr. Jinglehoffer's office. Looking up he saw Mr. Jinglehoffer standing in the doorway twirling his black moustache.

"What's on your mind, Chad?"

"Oh, hello, Mr. Jinglehoffer." Chad swallowed. He wondered if Mr. Jinglehoffer had seen him drop the red ball.

Mr. Jinglehoffer pulled at his watch fob. "Queenie and Sheba are making quite a racket this afternoon."

Chad nodded. "I'm going to find out what's the matter," he said, and hurried along.

The elephants trumpeted again. Chad could see them now. The great gray beasts were swaying from side to side and waving their long trunks in the air.

At the sight of Chad, Queenie and Sheba's wails changed to happy squeals. They began to dip their trunks in and out of the wooden drinking tub. Was the tub empty? Chad ran forward

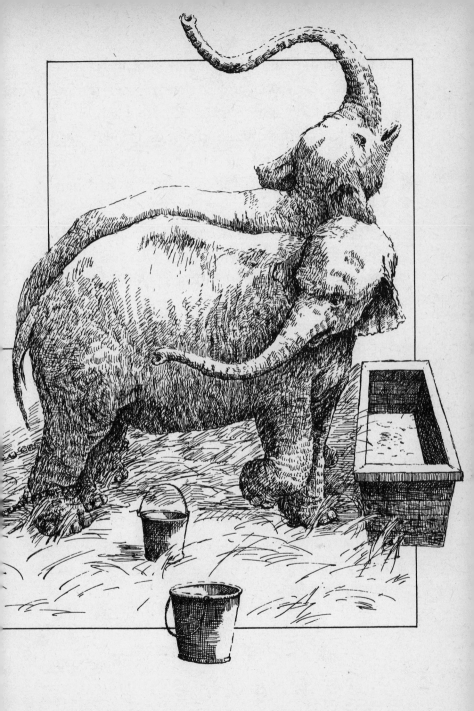

and looked. There was not a drop of water in it.

Chad just stood and looked. How strange! Subhas always saw to it that Queenie and Sheba had plenty to drink. Sometimes Chad helped bring water. He would carry half a bucket while Subhas carried two full ones. What had happened to Subhas?

Chad looked around. At last he spotted the trainer curled up under an old piece of canvas on a pile of hay behind the elephants. He was shivering and shaking.

Chad stared at his friend in alarm. "What's the matter, Subhas? Are you sick?"

Subhas nodded and pulled the canvas a little tighter.

Chad pointed at the elephants. "Did you know that Queenie and Sheba don't have any water?"

Subhas groaned. "No wonder they fuss. Find Rufe. He fill their tub."

Chad shook his head. "Rufe isn't here. I saw him going off toward town with some of the roustabouts."

Subhas sighed. "Oh, yes, I forget. I say this

24

morning he can go. But not mean before he do his work."

"Never mind, Subhas," Chad said. "I'll carry the water for Queenie and Sheba."

Subhas raised up on one elbow and then sank back. "If Sahib could! Only that too much for Chad alone. Maybe you find help."

"I can do it myself," Chad said and picked up the two buckets standing near the hay. "I can carry all the water Queenie and Sheba will need." He headed for the water pump.

It was hard work pushing the pump handle up and down. It was a long way from the pump to the elephants' big wooden tub. The buckets, only half full of water, seemed heavier each trip. Queenie and Sheba drank and drank and drank. Chad's hands began to grow sore and his arms ached.

At last Queenie and Sheba lifted their trunks from the tub of water and reached for a mouthful of hay. Chad dumped the last bucket of water in the tub and set the buckets on the ground with a sigh of relief. Queenie and Sheba had enough at last!

Chad looked at his hands. The bucket handles had rubbed blisters on his palms. He touched the red, tender skin. He felt tired all over, and hungry. He sniffed the air. The breeze carried the odor of good food from the cook tent. It was nearly suppertime.

Suddenly, Chad remembered his father's order to practice his juggling. He pulled the red, white, and blue balls from his pockets and began to toss them in the air. But his hands were stiff and sore. He dropped first one ball and then another. How would he ever juggle those balls tonight?

Chad stooped to pick up the white ball as the supper gong rang. He looked at Subhas still under the canvas on the hay.

"Come, Subhas, it's time for supper."

Subhas opened his eyes. "Go ahead. I come later." He raised his head. "*Saläm*, Sahib, for bringing the water to Queenie and Sheba."

"You're welcome." Chad looked anxiously at his friend. "If Doc is back from town, I'll send him around."

Doc owned the trained dog act in the show. He also tended both animals and people when

they were sick. He always seemed to know what doses of medicine to hand out from his big, old, black bag.

Chad put the balls in his pockets and headed for the cook tent. He would have to practice after supper. Maybe then his hands would feel better.

From
Bad to Worse

THE SUN HAD GONE DOWN behind the mountain peaks. Already the torches had been lighted on the circus grounds. Their yellow flames flickered in the breeze. Chad walked slowly toward his place in the parade line forming behind the main show-tent. He had changed to a green coat and pants and yellow vest.

He was glad to see Subhas with Rufe and the elephants. Subhas had wrapped himself in a purple robe. His head was covered with a golden turban. He looked shaky, but he had a smile for Chad.

"Doc come. Give bad medicine." Subhas made a wry face.

Rufe in a bright green turban and a dark yellow coat cast a sheepish look at Chad. "Thanks for the help."

Chad smiled. "Aw, it wasn't anything." He turned to the elephants who were squealing for attention. "Hi, Queenie and Sheba. Got your fancy trappings on, I see." He looked at the velvet blankets with golden fringe and tassels. Queenie's was royal purple and Sheba's emerald green.

Queenie stretched out her wrinkled trunk and with the tip softly brushed across Chad's hand.

Chad reached into his pocket. "You can't fool me, Queenie. I know what you're looking for." He pulled out a thick slice of bread. Queenie's trunk curled around the tidbit.

Sheba rumbled impatiently.

"I'm coming, Sheba." Chad hurried to where she stood behind Queenie. He reached into his other pocket. "Here's—hey there!" Before Chad could pull the bread halfway out, Sheba's trunk had snatched it from his pocket and moved it into her huge jaws.

"Better mind your manners, Sheba!" said Chad, laughing. "Now good-bye, both of you, until later."

Chad made his way to a yellow pony cart trimmed with green scrolls. The Shetland Pony's mane was braided with green rosettes. Chad patted her head. "Hi, Rosie. How are you tonight?" He stepped into the cart and took the reins.

Every circus performance began with the Grand Spectacular Parade that circled around the track inside the big show tent. Circus people had nicknamed it Spec. A roll of drums and a fanfare of trumpets brought everyone to attention.

The circus equestrian director in his tall, black, silk hat red coat, white breeches, and shiny, black boots stepped inside the tent. Chad could hear his voice rolling like low thunder.

"La-dies and Gen-tle-men! Pre-sen-ting the Jinglehoffer Circus Grand Spec-tac-u-lar Pa-rade!"

The clear ring of a bell sounded, and the band struck up the grand entry march. The line began to move. Chad could see the high-stepping white horse at the head of Spec. His rider wore a blue uniform, and an American flag waved over one shoulder. Behind him the band marched smartly along in their blue trousers and red coats. There were more horses and fancy-dressed riders.

Chad watched them step into the tent. Ahead of him the float with Sleeping Beauty and the Prince began to move.

"Giddy-up," said Chad, and Rosie walked forward.

All of the circus performers either marched or rode in Spec. Even the cook's helpers, the grooms, and other workers wore fancy costumes for the parade.

Rosie trotted into the tent. Every night Chad felt the same excitement. The tent was lighted with dozens of coal oil lanterns. Under their mellow glow, Spec with its glitter and bright

colors looked like a fairy tale come alive.

Children eating popcorn and peanuts shouted with delight. They waved to Chad and called out just as if they knew him. He held the reins with one hand and waved back with the other.

As Rosie pulled the yellow cart around the ring, Chad could see Dorinda and Don balancing on their white horses. He heard a roar of laughter and knew that Skeets and Rollo, the clowns, were doing crazy tricks.

Looking across the sawdust ring, Chad saw the wild animal cages entering, pulled by horses with red plumes behind their ears. There were lions in one, a tiger in another, and bears in a third.

Last of all came the elephants, huge and majestic in their gold-fringed velvet covers.

The band stepped out of line and took its place in the bandstand. The equestrian director was already at his station. He would direct the entire show with the sharp, clear ring of his little silver bell.

Chad and Rosie followed the Sleeping Beauty float out of the tent. Chad handed the reins to a waiting groom and climbed out of the cart. "See you tomorrow, Rosie," he said and headed for the pad room.

As he pulled off his green coat, Chad's sore arm muscles gave him a start. How was he ever going to get through those flying cartwheels? He shook his head and looked down at his blistered palms. Carefully he worked his fingers. He simply mustn't let one of those balls slip through his hands tonight.

Chad was wearing his acrobat tights underneath, so he was soon ready. The mountain night was cool, and he pulled on his jacket. Going outside, he watched the roustabouts packing away everything as soon as it was no longer needed. The cook tent had come down right after supper. The sideshow tents were disappearing.

Chad heard the band swing into "When Johnny Comes Marching Home." Inside the tent the dogs were marching on their hind legs. The acrobat act was next, and he hurried to the entrance.

There was the bell. Doc and his trained dogs

came running out as the acrobats went running in. Poppa was first. As he bounded into the ring, he flipped into a series of cartwheels that carried him around the sawdust circle. Carlos, Boots, and Mama followed, arms and legs flying.

Chad was last. He gritted his teeth and threw himself into a lopsided cartwheel. For an instant he was afraid he was going to fall flat on his face. With a painful jerk he saved himself and spun awkwardly on. Doggedly he made it around the circle.

No matter what happened, there was no time to pause. The band played on, and the music had been timed to fit—so many flip-flaps, hand-stands, somersaults, and balancing acts.

Chad's flip-flaps and somersaults were wobbly tonight. He hoped nobody noticed. On swung the music. It was time for Chad's special stunt.

Poppa crouched with his legs wide apart. Chad put his right foot on his father's knee. They clasped hands, and Chad, raising his left foot to Poppa's shoulder, mounted as Poppa swung him upward and straightened up.

Ouch! Chad's right hand was stinging. In

Chad tried to cover the blisters with his curled fingers, but his father saw them. He saw the raw spot where the skin had torn.

"No wonder you couldn't hold the balls! How on earth did you get these blisters?"

Queenie and Sheba moved out, gaily swinging their trunks. They were not tired. They did not mind that they still had to help take down the big show-tent.

Chad usually stayed to watch the end of the show, but not tonight. He buttoned on his red flannel shirt and brown breeches. He packed his costumes, banged shut the trunk lid, and snapped the locks. It was ready to be loaded into the trunk wagon.

A few torches lit a path across the field to the circus train. Tired and unhappy, Chad walked slowly along. Maybe he should have waited and ridden on one of the wagons. Yet he didn't want to see his father again tonight. At last he reached the train. His feet crunched along the cindery track to where the coaches stood.

Chad climbed aboard. No one else was in the sleeping car yet. Lanterns hung at either end of the coach and lighted the aisle with a dim glow. Chad crawled thankfully into his bunk. What a terrible day it had been. Tomorrow had to be better.

An Unexpected
Stop

CHAD SNUGGLED UNDER THE covers of his bunk in the circus train. He heard the wheels going clickety-clack, clickety-clack. *Acrobat boy, elephant boy, acrobat boy, elephant boy*, they seemed to be saying.

It was still dark in the sleeping car, since all of the curtains were drawn. Chad could see a crack of light along the edge of his window and knew it must be morning. He stretched first one arm and then the other. Not quite so stiff this morning. Carefully he spread his fingers. His hands were still sore, but better than last night.

He sat up remembering how cross his father had been. Why couldn't he be both an acrobat boy and an elephant boy?

Chad reached for the clothes he had placed in a pile at the end of his bunk. All of the other circus people were still asleep. They hardly ever went to bed before midnight and slept while the train traveled from one show place to the next. Chad's mother and father always slept as late as they could.

Not Chad. He liked to get up early—early for circus people, that is. He hurried into his red flannel shirt and pulled a sweater over it. The sleeping car was chilly in spite of a fire in the potbellied stove at one end. The circus was traveling high in the mountains, and it must be very cold outside.

Chad searched for his shoes and found them. Grabbing his jacket, he slid softly down from his bunk. Like a dark shadow he slipped down the aisle to the end of the car. The car swayed and the door was heavy, but he managed to open it. *Brrr!* It was freezing outside. He gripped the iron handrails. They were icy cold.

There was always a scary moment as he

stepped across the swaying metal plates that led to the next car. His eye saw a drift of snow on the mountainside. He pushed hard on the door and squeezed inside.

The far end of the car was for baggage, but this end had several small tables and chairs. There was an iron stove and a cabinet with a work space. Circus people called this the pie car. After the show and when they were moving, they could gather here for a piece of pie or a sandwich and a cup of coffee. They could play card games, or sit and visit.

Chad was not surprised to find the pie car empty so early in the morning. Empty and cold. The fire in the stove had burned down to a bed of ash-covered coals. He blew and the coals glowed red. There was plenty of wood stacked handy and a basket of chips. Soon Chad had a good blaze going. He warmed his hands and pulled up a chair.

Through the window he could see the mountain slopes of evergreen forests and huge rock cliffs. The train puffed along. On one side the huge, jagged rocks stretched up and up. On the

other side the rocky slope dropped down and
down.

Clickety-clack, clickety-clack. He heard the
wheels speaking to him again. *Acrobat boy, elephant boy, acrobat boy, elephant boy.* Why
couldn't he be *both* an acrobat boy and an ele-

47

phant boy? A fearful thought caught him. What if his father wouldn't let him work with the elephants anymore?

Chad stared out of the train window and tried not to think about such an awful thing. He could see the narrow tracks winding back and forth up the mountain in big S curves. He saw the circus train's red engine pulling slowly around the curve ahead. Big clouds of black smoke were puffing from its broad smokestack. Behind the engine and wood-filled tender trailed the string of yellow circus cars.

First came the stock cars with the horses and elephants. Next were the flatcars bearing the wagons and wild-animal cages. The coaches for the people were last of all.

Chad put another stick of wood in the stove and banged the iron door shut. Could Poppa take him out of the elephant act? Mr. Jingle-hoffer always had the final say-so, but Poppa was a powerful talker.

The train was climbing through a forest. It pulled over a bridge that crossed a mountain stream. Down below Chad saw heavy timbers framing the dark hole of a tunnel and a rough shack nearby. Was it a gold or silver mine? he wondered.

A man stepped out of the shack, grinned, and waved. Chad waved back.

Higher and higher climbed the train, moving more and more slowly. Chad could hear the engine huffing and puffing as loudly as ever, but slower—slower—*stop*!

The train halted with a jerk and a clankety, clank, clank, clank that went from the first car to the next and all the way back to the very last one—c l a n k, c l a n k. It was enough, thought Chad, to wake everybody up.

He peered out of the windows first on one side and then on the other. No town, no buildings, not even a railroad siding. He put his face against the window. Why had they stopped here? he wondered. He saw the conductor running alongside the tracks up ahead and heard someone shouting.

What could be the matter? At that moment Mr. Jinglehoffer ran past the window, his black moustache twitching. Something must have happened!

At once Chad jumped to his feet and ran to the end of the car. He pulled the door open and stepped out into the freezing air. He leaped down the steps, buttoning his jacket as he went. He pulled his stocking cap out of his pocket and tugged it down over his ears as he raced along the tracks after Mr. Jinglehoffer.

Up ahead Chad could see the conductor talking to the engineer and the fireman. White steam hissed from the engine.

Mr. Jinglehoffer strode up to the engineer. "Why have we stopped here?" he demanded. "What's the matter?"

The engineer stood with his feet wide apart and shook his head. "Your circus train is too heavy. My engine can't pull you over the mountain."

Acrobat Boy,
Elephant Boy

MR. JINGLEHOFFER STOOD with his mouth hanging open. He looked at the engineer as if he couldn't believe his ears. Then he found his voice. "Can't pull us over the mountain! Why, we're almost at the top now."

The engineer nodded. "I know. But what's left is the steepest grade on the run. Your train is too heavy."

Mr. Jinglehoffer waved his hands wildly. "We have to get to Leadville. We have posters up— a show today."

The engineer planted his feet more firmly.

"I'm sorry. Your train is *too* heavy."

Mr. Jinglehoffer's black moustache shook fiercely in the wind. "We can't just sit here on this mountain! We'll all freeze to death!"

Chad pulled his collar tighter around his neck and nodded.

The engineer was shivering, too. "There's only one thing to do. We've got to back down the mountain."

"Back down the mountain!" Mr. Jinglehoffer shook his fist. "No! My circus has to get to Leadville this morning. Surely your train has pulled heavier loads than this."

The engineer snorted. "Of course—mining machinery, gold and silver ore, coal, and heavy timbers. But we've always had another engine to push from behind."

Mr. Jinglehoffer smiled with relief. "Another engine! Of course. Why didn't I think of that? We'll get another engine to push."

The engineer still shook his head. "We have to back down the mountain to the last town, telegraph for a second engine, and then wait for it to come."

"That will make us too late," wailed Mr.

Jinglehoffer. "We must get there soon."

Suddenly Chad remembered something. He tugged at Mr. Jinglehoffer's sleeve. "Mr. Jinglehoffer—"

Mr. Jinglehoffer paid no attention. He turned to the fireman. "Can't you build a bigger fire and get up more steam?"

The fireman pointed to the steam still hissing from the engine. "We have a full head of steam, but it's not enough."

"That's right," said the engineer.

"That's right," said the conductor.

Chad tugged Mr. Jinglehoffer's sleeve again. "Please, sir, I know what we could do."

Mr. Jinglehoffer glared at the engineer, the fireman, and the conductor. "If the grade is so steep, why didn't the Denver, South Park & Pacific Railroad give us two engines in the first place?"

This time Chad did not tug at Mr. Jinglehoffer's sleeve. Instead, he jumped right between the circus manager and the engineer. "Queenie and Sheba, Queenie and Sheba! They can do it!" he shouted.

The engineer's bushy eyebrows raised in surprise.

Mr. Jinglehoffer's moustache bristled. "Queenie and Sheba can do what?"

"Queenie and Sheba can be the second engine that pushes the train over the mountain."

The engineer's bushy black brows shot up in surprise again. "An elephant engine?"

Mr. Jinglehoffer's moustache was waving with excitement. "Why, of course. An elephant engine! The elephants often push circus wagons out of the mud. They can push the train!"

"Huh!" scoffed the conductor. "Up that steep grade? Impossible!"

"How far would they have to push?" asked Mr. Jinglehoffer.

The engineer pointed ahead. "Up to the hump would do it."

Mr. Jinglehoffer measured the distance with his eye. "It's our only hope. We'll try it." He turned to the little crowd of circus people that had gathered around and saw Rufe. "Wake up Subhas, Rufe, and tell him to lead the elephants out of their car at once."

Rufe shook his head. "I'm sorry, Mr. Jingle-hoffer, but Subhas is sick. He wouldn't last two minutes out in this cold."

"That's right," spoke up Doc.

Mr. Jinglehoffer groaned. "The elephants are our only chance." He pointed a finger at Rufe. "You're the new bull hand. You'll have to do it."

Rufe pulled back, shaking his head. "Not me! Sorry, sir. I'm so new I haven't learned that Indian lingo yet. I don't know the commands. The best I could do is help."

"Sufferin' cats and dogs!" bellowed Mr. Jinglehoffer. "What good is a bull hand who can't handle his elephants?"

Rufe looked wildly around. His eye lighted on Chad. "The kid here could do it. He knows the commands, and the elephants are used to him."

Mr. Jinglehoffer looked at Chad. "What about it? Could you handle Queenie and Sheba?"

Chad suddenly had a funny feeling in the pit of his stomach. Hadn't he told himself a hundred times that he was big enough to handle Queenie and Sheba? Only he had supposed Subhas would

be there, too. Without Subhas . . . Still, the
train had to get over the mountain.

Chad looked at Mr. Jinglehoffer. He looked
at Rufe. He looked at the silent group watching

him and saw his father. Poppa gave a little nod.

Chad turned back to Mr. Jinglehoffer. "I think Queenie and Sheba would work for me. I'll try."

"That's the spirit!" cheered Mr. Jinglehoffer, taking Chad's hand. He turned to the others. "Some of you come along and help. The rest of you folks get everyone else off the train. We'll make the load as light as we can. Come on, Chad, let's go."

Together they hurried to the elephant car. Rufe and several of the roustabouts followed. Poppa came, too. Poppa who never paid any attention to the elephants.

Rufe found the thick pads that the elephants wore for pushing.

Chad gave the orders. "*Seer*, Queenie, *seer*." The elephant lowered her head, and Rufe and Chad strapped on the pad.

"*Seer*, Sheba, *seer*." They buckled Sheba's pad in place.

Poppa and the roustabouts had pulled out the heavy wooden ramp and shoved it into place at the car door. There was barely enough room

for it along the right of way.

Queenie stuck her trunk out the door into the cold wind. Quickly she brought it in again.

Chad, gripping the bull hook, stood beside Queenie's left front leg. "*Utthao*, Queenie." He tried to give the order to move ahead in exactly the same tone Subhas used.

Queenie rolled an eye at him, but she didn't budge.

Chad spoke in a louder voice. "*Utthao*, Queenie."

Queenie flapped her ears, but she didn't move her legs.

Chad looked at the bull hook in his hand, and he looked at the elephant towering above him. "Queenie, I know you don't like that cold wind, but this is something that has to be done." Then as Chad gave the order, he prodded Queenie with the bull hook. "*Utthao, utthao*."

Queenie gave a little rumble as if to say, *So you really mean business*. Then she lifted her thick gray legs and moved slowly down the ramp with Chad close beside her.

It was a tight squeeze at the bottom, but for

all her great size, Queenie could swing those big feet in a very, narrow space.

When they had cleared the ramp, Chad stopped. He looked back at the elephant car where Rufe waited with Sheba. "*Utthao*, Sheba," ordered Chad. Rufe poked with his bull hook, and Sheba followed Queenie.

Down the length of the train they tramped. Past the stock cars, past the flatcars with the wagons and wild-animal cages. Past the coaches where the circus people rode.

Mr. Jinglehoffer, Poppa, the roustabouts, and the conductor trailed behind. At the end of the train, Chad turned the elephants onto the track.

"*Udhar jao*, Queenie. *Udhar jao*, Sheba. . . . *Utthao*, Queenie. *Utthao*, Sheba." Finally the elephants stood behind the last yellow coach. Roustabouts had already removed the iron hand rail.

"Queenie a little more this way," shouted Poppa.

"Sheba a little more that way," shouted Mr. Jinglehoffer.

"*Idhar ao*, Queenie. *Udhar jao*, Sheba,"

ordered Chad, and the elephants did as he said.

"Good! Good!" shouted both Poppa and Mr. Jinglehoffer.

The conductor stood out to one side where

he could be seen by the engineer leaning out of the cab window way up the track.

"All set?" asked Mr. Jinglehoffer.

"Ready," said Chad.

"Ready," said Rufe.

"Ready," said the conductor. With a wave of his arm he told the engineer to open the throttle.

"*Dhakka lagao*, Queenie and Sheba. *Dhakka lagao*," ordered Chad as he prodded with the bull hook.

The elephants bent their great heads and pushed. Nothing happened.

The conductor sniffed. "I said it wouldn't work."

"Push harder, Queenie," said Chad. "*Dhakka lagao*, *beti*. That's it, Sheba. *Dhakka lagao!* I know you can do it. *Dhakka lagao!*"

Queenie and Sheba braced their great shoulders and pushed and pushed and pushed. Slowly, slowly the wheels of the cars began to turn.

"We're moving!" shouted Mr. Jinglehoffer.

The conductor shook his head. "They'll never keep it up."

Poppa jabbed his fist in the air as if that would help. "Keep pushing! Keep pushing!"

"*Dhakka lagao, dhakka lagao*, Queenie and Sheba," urged Chad.

Round and round rolled the train wheels, up and up the incline. Queenie and Sheba were breathing hard.

"We're almost to the top," shouted Poppa.

"Just a little farther, Queenie and Sheba, just a little farther," implored Mr. Jinglehoffer.

Chad was breathing hard, too. He had forgotten the cold. The elephants must keep pushing. *"Dhakka lagao, beti. Dhakka lagao."*

He heard Rufe mutter, "Push, Sheba, baby. Don't stop now."

At that moment the train pulled ahead on its own power and chugged over the hump. Queenie and Sheba had done it. They had pushed the train up the steepest grade on the mountain. A cheer rose from all the circus people who had walked up the tracks behind the elephant engine.

"*Bahut accha*, Queenie and Sheba, *bahut accha*," praised Chad. "Well done."

The conductor stood shaking his head. "If I hadn't seen it myself, I never would have believed it."

Mr. Jinglehoffer was waving his hands with excitement. "You did it! You did it! Subhas himself couldn't have done better. What can I do for you, Chad? Just name it."

"Oh, Mr. Jinglehoffer," cried Chad, "do you think—do you think maybe I could see the stores in Leadville? I hear it's a really big town."

"You shall see them if I have to hitch up a wagon and take you myself," promised Mr. Jinglehoffer.

People were hurrying up and into the warmth of the coaches.

Carlos and Boots paused for a moment to thump Chad on the back. "You were tops. Absolutely tops."

Chad looked around. Where was Poppa? Where was Mama? They were nowhere in sight. Chad turned slowly back to the elephants.

Queenie and Sheba stood with their sides heaving. Little puffs of steam came from their trunks. Chad gave Queenie a pat on the side. "*Bahut accha*, Queenie *beti*. Well done, Queenie baby."

Queenie stretched out her trunk and gently

rubbed across Chad's hand with the tip.

Rufe reached up and patted Sheba behind the ears. "Good work, baby, good work."

Chad grinned at Rufe. "Time to get the elephants back on the train. "*Udhar jao*, Queenie."

Rufe grinned back at Chad. "*Udhar jao*, Sheba," he ordered.

Chad gasped with astonishment. "Rufe, you did it! You gave Sheba the order in Hindi."

Rufe blinked with surprise. "Rolled right off my tongue. Doesn't sound strange anymore."

Chad sat at a table in the pie car and took a bite of cheese sandwich. The car was full of people talking and laughing. Everyone wanted to speak to Chad.

Chad smiled at his circus friends. "Thanks," he said again and again. "Rufe helped, too, but it was really Queenie and Sheba who did the work."

Rufe had not come to the pie car. "I gotta see that Queenie and Sheba are all right," he had told Chad. "A bull hand has to take care of his elephants."

69

Chad took another bite of his sandwich and tried to sort out his thoughts. It had been exciting to give the orders to Queenie and Sheba, but he was glad he didn't have to stay back in the elephant car with them.

Chad's eyes moved to the door. Suddenly it opened, letting in a *whish* of cold air. Mama, pretty in her her long blue cloak, stepped inside. Poppa, tall and strong, was behind her. People moved aside to let them through to where Chad sat.

Mama bent over with a kiss. "Oh, Chad, we're so proud of you."

Poppa cleared his throat. "I'm sorry that I wasn't around to help get the elephants back in the car. I didn't mean to run off. I turned around to find Mama. She wasn't anywhere in the crowd. I couldn't figure out what had happened to her."

Mama's laugh rang like little bells. "Poppa didn't know that I never got off the train. I was fixing coffee, and I wanted to take Subhas a cup. The train was rolling before I knew it. Subhas feels a little better. He said to tell you, '*Saläm*, Sahib.'"

Poppa took a deep breath. "Mama, I wish you could have seen Chad making Queenie go down that ramp. And you should have seen those elephants push when Chad said push."

Mama kissed Chad again. "Oh, Chad, those great big elephants! How did you ever do it?"

Chad shrugged. "I just talked to Queenie and Sheba the way Subhas does."

Mama looked up at Poppa. "See! Chad wasn't fooling around when he visited the elephants. He was learning to talk to them. All those Indian words! Smart boy we have, Poppa."

Poppa raised an eyebrow. "Smart elephants, Mama—and willing to work."

Mama shook her head and blinked her long lashes at Poppa. "Now, Poppa, you know perfectly well that without Chad to give the orders, Queenie and Sheba wouldn't have been any help at all."

A little smile began under Poppa's walrus moustache. "Mebbe so, mebbe so, Mama." He sucked in a deep breath and his chest rose. "Haven't I always said we're the best acrobat family in the business?" Poppa looked down at

Chad. "If he puts his mind to it, our boy might even be a top juggler some day."

"Oh, Poppa!" scolded Mama. "You know you're all but bursting your buttons." She patted Chad's shoulders. "We're proud of you, son."

Poppa put an arm around Mama. "How about a quick cup of coffee? We'll soon be in Leadville."

Chad stared at Poppa's broad back moving toward the coffeepot. He was thinking back. Queenie and Sheba hadn't wanted to go out in the cold wind. It had taken every ounce of their great strength to push so hard. But they had done it.

Chad took another bite of sandwich. Clickety clack, clickety clack went the train wheels. *Acrobat boy, elephant boy, acrobat boy.* Chad's fingers crept into his jacket pocket. They closed over two round balls. He crammed the last bite of sandwich into his mouth.

People were clearing out of the pie car. Chad saw an empty corner and headed for it. He pulled the red and white balls from his left pocket and the blue ball from his right pocket. What did it matter if his hands were a little sore? He couldn't let the best acrobat family in the business down.

Clickety clack, clickety clack. In spite of the swaying motion of the train, he planted his feet firmly. With a flick of his fingers, Chad sent the red ball, the white ball, and the blue ball into the air.